OVER the RIVER
A Turkey's Tale

Derek Anderson

based on the song by Lydia Maria Child

Simon & Schuster Books for Young Readers

New York   London   Toronto   Sydney

for Alyssa—D. A.

SIMON & SCHUSTER BOOKS FOR YOUNG READERS
An imprint of Simon & Schuster Children's Publishing Division
1230 Avenue of the Americas, New York, New York 10020
Text copyright © 2005 by Simon & Schuster, Inc.
Illustrations copyright © 2005 by Derek Anderson
All rights reserved, including the right of reproduction in whole or in part in
any form.
SIMON & SCHUSTER BOOKS FOR YOUNG READERS is a trademark of Simon & Schuster, Inc.
Book design by Daniel Roode
The text for this book is set in Fontoon.
The illustrations for this book are rendered in acrylic paint.
"Over the River" arranged by Donald P. Moore, copyright © 1988 by
Fotsco Music Press, a division of Shawnee Press, Inc. (ASCAP)
International copyright secured. All rights reserved.
Reprinted by permission. Arrangement adapted by Dan Sovak © 2005
Manufactured in the United States of America
10 9 8 7 6 5
Library of Congress Cataloging-in-Publication Data
Anderson, Derek, 1969-
Over the river: a turkey's tale / adapted and illustrated by Derek
Anderson.— 1st ed.
p. cm.
From the poem by Lydia Maria Child.
Summary: Presents the words to the popular Thanksgiving song,
with illustrations of a turkey family going to Grandma and Grandpa
Turkey's house, pursued by a boy and a dog who are hunting for
Thanksgiving dinner.
ISBN-13: 978-0-689-87635-6
ISBN-10:   0-689-87635-1
1. Thanksgiving Day—Songs and music. 2. Children's songs—Texts.
[1. Thanksgiving Day—Songs and music. 2. Songs.] I. Title.
PZ8.3.A5453Ov 2005
782.42164'0268—dc22   2004018305
Based on the song "Over the River the River and Through the
Woods" by Lydia Maria Child.
0911 PCR

to Grandmother's house we go.

The horse knows the way
to carry the sleigh

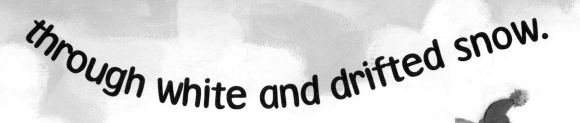

through white and drifted snow.

Over the river and through the woods,

oh, how the wind does blow!

It stings the toes and bites the nose,

as over the ground we go.

Over the river and through the woods,

to have a first-rate play.

Oh,
hear
the
bell
RING,

ting-
a-
ling-
ling,

hurrah for Thanksgiving Day!

Over the river and through the woods,

spring over the ground

for this is Thanksgiving Day.

Over the River

by Lydia Maria Child